Disney
ZOOTOPIA

THE JUNIOR NOVELIZATION

randomhousekids.com

ISBN 978-0-7364-3394-5

Printed in the United States of America

10 9 8 7 6 5 4 3 2 1

ZOOTOPIA

THE JUNIOR NOVELIZATION

Adapted by Suzanne Francis

Random House 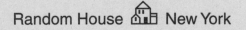 New York

The wild sounds of ancient predators echoed through a large barn in Bunnyburrow. A young bunny named Judy Hopps appeared on a makeshift stage, trying to find her way through a papier-mâché and cardboard jungle.

Judy's voice rang out loud and clear. "Fear. Treachery. Bloodlust! Thousands of years ago, these were the forces that ruled our world. A world where prey were scared of predators. And predators had an uncontrollable desire to maim and maul and—"

Suddenly, a jaguar leapt on her from the shadows!

"Blood, blood, blood!" Judy screamed as she crumpled under the attack. "And death."

After a long and drawn-out moment of terrible silence, Judy sat up, faced the confused audience, and smiled as she continued her monologue. A banner reading CARROT DAYS TALENT SHOW hung over the stunned crowd.

"Back then, the world was divided in two: vicious predator or meek prey." Two cardboard boxes dropped down from the ceiling. The first, labeled VICIOUS PREDATOR in crayon, landed on top of the jaguar, and the second, labeled MEEK PREY, landed on Judy. The boxes settled on their shoulders so their heads, arms, and legs stuck out. "But over time, we evolved and moved beyond our primitive, savage ways."

A young sheep wearing a white robe and a cardboard rainbow on his head did an improvisational dance across the stage. Judy and the jaguar burst out of their boxes, now wearing white robes, too. "Now predator and prey live in harmony."

Judy and the jaguar, revealed as another friendly youngster, shook hands as the sheep sprinkled glitter on them. "And every young mammal has multitudinous opportunities," Judy said.

"Yeah. I don't have to cower in a herd anymore," said the sheep. Then he ripped off his robe, revealing a homemade astronaut costume. "Instead, I can be an astronaut."

"I don't have to grow up to be a lonely hunter," said the jaguar, showing a business suit under his robe.

"Today I can hunt for tax exemptions. I'm gonna be an actuary!"

"And no longer do I have to blindly serve the almighty carrot," said Judy. "I can make the world a better place—saving lives, defending the defenseless! I am going to be . . ." Judy ripped off her robe and stood in a blue uniform. "A police officer!"

In the audience, a nasty fox kid named Gideon Grey snickered to his two friends. "Bunny cop. That is the most stupidest thing I ever heard," he said.

Back onstage, it was almost as if Judy had heard his remark. "It may seem impossible . . . to small minds," she said, pointing at him. "I'm looking at you, Gideon Grey." Judy snapped her fingers and a backdrop showing a bright city skyline unrolled behind her. "But just two hundred and eleven miles away stands the great city of . . . ZOOTOPIA! Where our ancestors first joined together in peace. And declared that Anyone Can Be Anything! Thank you and good night!"

Judy proudly bowed, as if she had just given the performance of her life. Dutiful applause came from the audience, including her parents, Bonnie and Stu Hopps.

Moments later, Judy, still wearing her police

costume, excitedly exited the barn with her parents. Outside, the Carrot Days Festival was in full swing as everyone enjoyed booths, games, and rides.

"Judy, ever wonder how your mom and me got to be so darn happy?" Stu asked.

"Nope," Judy answered.

"Well, I'll tell ya how," Stu continued, as if he hadn't heard Judy. "We gave up on our dreams and we settled, right, Bon?"

"Oh yes," Bonnie agreed. "That's right, Stu. We settled hard."

"See, that's the beauty of complacency, Jude. If you don't try anything new, you'll never fail," Stu said.

"I like trying, actually," Judy said.

Bonnie looked at their daughter. "What your father means, hon . . . it's gonna be difficult—impossible, even—for you to become a police officer."

"There's never been a bunny cop," Stu said.

"I guess I'll have to be the first one!" said Judy as she parkoured against a fence. "Because I'm gonna make the world a better place."

"Or . . . heck, you wanna talk about making the world a better place—no better way to do it than becoming a carrot farmer," said Stu.

"Yes! Your dad and me and your two hundred

seventy-five brothers and sisters—we're changing the world one carrot at a time," said Bonnie.

"Amen to that. Carrot farming is a noble profession," Stu agreed.

But Judy stopped paying attention to her parents when she spotted Gideon Grey following some little kids. She was instantly alert, and she went after him.

"You get it, honey?" Bonnie asked Judy. "I mean, it's great to have dreams."

"Yeah, just as long as you don't believe in them too much," Stu continued as he looked around for his daughter. "Jude? Where the heck did she go?"

2

Judy got closer and saw Gideon Grey doing what the fox did best—bullying some kids.

"Give me your tickets right now, or I'm gonna kick your meek little sheep butt," said Gideon, before giving the kid a shove. Then he took the sheep's tickets and smacked her with them. "Baa-baa," he mocked. "What're ya gonna do, cry?"

"Ow!" yelped the sheep. "Cut it out, Gideon!"

"Hey!" said Judy firmly. "You heard her. Cut it out."

Gideon looked at Judy and laughed. "Nice costume, loser," he snarled. "What crazy world are you living in where you think a bunny could be a cop?"

"Kindly return my friend's tickets," Judy said calmly.

Gideon snarled and stuffed the tickets into his pocket. "Come get 'em. But watch out, 'cause I'm a fox. And like you said in your dumb little stage play, us predators used to eat prey. And that killer instinct is still in our Dunnahh."

"I'm pretty sure it's pronounced D-N-A," whispered one of Gideon's wolf pals.

"Don't tell me what I know, Travis," Gideon said, irritated.

"You don't scare me, Gideon," said Judy.

Gideon shoved Judy so hard that she fell to the ground with a thud. Judy's eyes began to water.

"You scared now?" Gideon said cruelly. The other prey animals cowered behind a tree, leaving Judy to face the bullies alone.

"Look at her nose twitch," said Travis mockingly. "She *is* scared!"

"Cry, little baby bunny. Cry, cry—" Gideon taunted.

Bam! Before Gideon could say another word, Judy kicked him in the face with her hind legs, knocking him down. But he sprang right back up, and he was mad. "Oh, you don't know when to quit, do you?" Gideon said, unsheathing his claws like a fist of knives.

He slapped Judy in the face, his sharp claws digging into her skin, making her bleed. Then he knocked her down and held her face in the dirt. "I want you to remember this moment," Gideon said coldly, "anytime you think you'll ever be anything more than just a stupid, carrot-farming dumb bunny."

Gideon and his pals walked away, laughing, leaving Judy in the dirt. She got up, wiped the blood off her cheek, and glared at their backs.

"Aw jeez, that looks bad," said Gareth, a sheep.

"Are you okay, Judy?" asked Sharla, the sheep the bullies had taken the tickets from.

Judy took a breath and pulled something out of her front pocket, smiling wide.

"Here you go!" she said, returning the tickets that Gideon had stolen.

"Wicked! You got our tickets!" said Sharla.

"You're awesome, Judy!" exclaimed Gareth.

"That Gideon Grey doesn't know what he's talking about," Sharla added.

Judy slapped her police hat back on top of her head, and there was a look of determination in her eye. "Well, he was right about one thing: I don't know when to quit."

Fifteen years later, Judy Hopps worked her tail off in the Zootopia Police Academy. She was small compared to the rest of the cadets—who were mostly elephants, rhinos, and bison—but she was strong-willed.

Because of her size, the physical training was the toughest part. Cadets had to get through obstacles in simulators that mimicked all of the twelve unique ecosystems that made up the city of Zootopia. From freezing Tundratown to sweltering Sahara Square, each ecosystem presented its own set of challenges—whether it was trying to scale an ice wall or survive in a scorching sandstorm.

Judy fell down more than anyone. In her mind she could hear the voices of her parents, her drill instructor, and Gideon Grey all doubting that there could ever be a bunny cop. And it was those voices that made Judy work harder than anyone else. Through persistence and perseverance, she managed to keep up and surprise everyone.

In the final weeks of training, Judy used her bunny skills, like her strong legs and her great hearing, to help prove her worth. She sailed through the physical obstacles and at times even passed the other cadets. Once, she knocked down a male rhino ten times her size during a final sparring session!

On graduation day, Judy took her place among the other graduates during the ceremony, including the rhino who sported a fat lip and a black eye. The mayor, a lion named Leodore Lionheart, stepped up to the podium.

"As mayor of Zootopia, I am proud to announce that my Mammal Inclusion Initiative has produced its first police academy graduate. The valedictorian of her class . . . ZPD's very first rabbit police officer, Judy Hopps. Assistant Mayor Bellwether, her badge?" the mayor said to a small sheep standing nearby.

"Oh! Yes. Right," said Bellwether.

"Judy, it is my great privilege to officially assign you to the heart of Zootopia: Precinct One, City Center," Lionheart said.

Judy walked across the stage to the sound of

deafening applause—the loudest coming from her parents, even as Stu sobbed.

Mayor Lionheart handed Judy her diploma while Bellwether stepped forward and pinned her ZPD badge onto her uniform. "Congratulations, Officer Hopps."

"I won't let you down. This has been my dream since I was a kid," said Judy.

"It's a real proud day for us little guys," Bellwether whispered.

"Bellwether, make room, will you?" said Lionheart, smiling broadly. "All right, Officer Hopps. Let's see those teeth!"

A photographer posed Judy with Mayor Lionheart and Bellwether. But Lionheart edged Bellwether out of the photo.

Days later, Judy's parents, along with several siblings, accompanied her to the train station.

"We're real proud of you, Judy," said Bonnie.

"Yeah. Scared, too," said Stu. "Really, it's a proud-scared combo. I mean, Zootopia. It's so far away and such a big city."

"Guys, I've been working for this my whole life," Judy told her parents, trying to hide how thrilled she really was.

"We know," said Bonnie. "And we're just a little excited for you, but terrified."

"'The only thing we have to fear is fear itself,'" said Judy.

"And also bears," said Stu. "We have bears to fear, too. To say nothing of lions, wolves . . ."

"Wolves?" Bonnie asked, perplexed.

". . . weasels . . . ," Stu continued.

"You play cribbage with a weasel," said Bonnie.

"And he cheats like there's no tomorrow. Pretty much all predators do—and Zootopia's full of 'em. And foxes are the worst."

"Actually, your father does have a point there," added Bonnie. "It's in their biology. Remember what happened with Gideon Grey?"

"When I was nine," said Judy. "Gideon Grey was a jerk who happened to be a fox. I know plenty of bunnies who are jerks."

"Sure. We all do. Absolutely," said Stu. "But just in case, we made you a little care package to take with you." He held out a bag.

"And I put some snacks in there," said Bonnie.

Judy looked inside and saw a bunch of pink spray canisters.

"This is fox repellent," explained Stu, picking one up.

"Yeah, that's safe to have," said Bonnie.

"This is fox deterrent . . . ," Stu said, pointing at something that looked like an air horn.

"The deterrent and the repellent. That's all she needs," Bonnie said, trying to stop Stu from going overboard.

"Check this out!" Stu said as he pulled out a fox Taser and turned it on, causing it to sizzle.

"Oh, for goodness' sake! She has no need for a fox Taser, Stu."

"Come on. When is there not a need for a fox Taser?" asked Stu.

"Okay, I will take this to make you stop talking," said Judy. She grabbed the pink can of fox repellent as the train approached.

"Terrific! Everyone wins!" Stu exclaimed.

"Arriving! Zootopia express!" called the conductor.

"Okay. Gotta go. Bye!" said Judy, heading for the train.

Stu and Bonnie held back tears as they watched their daughter walk off. Suddenly, Judy turned back and ran to her parents. She wrapped her arms around them both. "I love you guys," she said, hugging them.

"Love you, too!" said Bonnie.

After one more hug, Judy jumped onto the train.

"Cripes, here come the waterworks," said Stu as his tears started to flow. *"Ahhahoho jeesh . . ."*

"Oh, Stu, pull it together," whispered Bonnie.

The big crowd of bunnies watched Judy go, and as the train pulled away, they ran next to it, waving and shouting their goodbyes.

"Bye, everybody! Bye!" Judy called.

When their faces faded into the distance, Judy climbed to the observation deck and took a deep breath. She pulled out her phone and clicked on some music, feeling like her life was about to begin.

4

As the train came around a bend, Judy gazed out the window at the incredible sight in the distance: Zootopia. She pressed her face against the glass and watched each borough of the city pass by.

Judy exited the train at Central Station, which served downtown Zootopia, and made her way outside into the city's central plaza. It was incredible! She took out her earbuds and let the chaotic city sounds wash over her as she looked around, awestruck. Animals of all shapes and sizes rushed by, hurrying this way and that. It was a far cry from Bunnyburrow!

She looked down at her phone and checked her maps app to figure out which way to go.

When she found her apartment building, the landlady, Dharma, an armadillo, led her to a little apartment.

"Welcome to the Grand Pangolin Arms," said

Dharma, stepping aside to let Judy in. "Complimentary delousing once a month. Don't lose your key."

Kudu and Oryx, Judy's neighbors, passed in the hallway. Judy greeted them warmly. "Oh, hi, I'm Judy. Your new neighbor."

"Yeah, well, we're loud," said Kudu.

"Don't expect us to apologize for it," added Oryx.

The two hurried off, slamming the door of their apartment behind them. Dharma had left as well, leaving Judy alone in her apartment for the first time. She looked around.

"Greasy walls . . . rickety bed . . . ," said Judy.

Then loud voices came from the other side of the wall: "Shut up!" "You shut up!" "No! You shut up!"

"Crazy neighbors." Judy flopped onto the bed with a big smile. "I *love* it!"

5

Beep. Beep. Beep. At the sound of her morning alarm, Judy sprang out of bed. She washed, brushed, and rinsed. Then she put on her vest, pinned on her badge, and strapped on her belt. She was ready to protect the city! She glanced at the pink can of fox repellent sitting on the bedside table and walked out, leaving it behind. But after a moment, she reached back in the room and grabbed it—just in case.

She left her apartment and headed toward the Zootopia Police Department for her first day on the job!

Judy's eyes widened as she entered the chaotic and loud ZPD. Big burly cops pushed criminals through the lobby as people rushed around in every direction. She dodged a few husky animals before finally finding her way to the front desk. There, a pudgy, friendly-looking cheetah sat chatting with some other cops.

Judy smiled at him as she approached, but he couldn't see her because she was shorter than the desk.

"Excuse me!" Judy called up to the desk. "Down here. Down. *Here*. Hi."

The cheetah leaned over the desk and saw Judy standing there in her uniform.

"O-M goodness!" he said. "They really did hire a bunny. What! I gotta tell you; you are even cuter than I thought you'd be."

Judy winced. "Oh, uh, I'm sure you didn't know, but for us rabbits . . . the word 'cute' is a—it's a little—"

"Oh! I am so sorry. *Me*, Benjamin Clawhauser, the guy everyone thinks is just a flabby, donut-loving cop, stereotyping *you* . . . ," he said apologetically.

"It's okay. Oh, um, actually you've—actually—" Judy stammered as she tried to figure out how to say it. "There's a—in your neck—the fold . . . there's—"

Clawhauser removed a small donut from under a roll of neck fat. "There you went, you little dickens!" said Clawhauser to the donut. Then he joyfully crammed it into his mouth.

"I should get to roll call, so . . . which way do I . . . ?" Judy asked.

"Oh!" Clawhauser said with his mouth full of

donut. "Bullpen's over there to the left."

"Great, thank you!" Judy said, and hurried off.

"Aw . . . that poor little bunny's gonna get eaten alive," he said, watching her go.

Inside the bullpen, rhinos, buffalo, hippos, and elephants prepared for work. They towered over Judy, but she didn't mind. She excitedly climbed up into a massive, elephant-sized chair and gazed around the room.

"Hey. Officer Hopps," Judy extended her paw to a gigantic rhino whose name tag read MCHORN. "You ready to make the world a better place?" she asked sincerely.

McHorn snorted and reluctantly gave her a fist bump, nearly knocking her off her chair.

"TEN-HUT!" shouted one of the officers as Police Chief Bogo, a gruff Cape buffalo, entered the room. Everyone instantly fell in line and started stomping on the floor.

"All right, all right. Everybody sit," said Bogo. "I've got three items on the docket. First, we need to acknowledge the elephant in the room." He nodded toward an elephant officer. "Francine, happy birthday."

The shy elephant blushed as the cops clapped,

snorted, and hooted. "Number two: there are some new recruits with us I should introduce. But I'm not going to, because I don't care."

Bogo moved toward a map. "Finally, we have fourteen missing mammal cases," he said, gesturing to the pushpin-covered map. "FOURTEEN CASES. Now, that's more than we've ever had, and City Hall is right up my tail to solve them. This is priority one. Assignments!"

Bogo began barking out assignments as one of the officers handed out case files. "Officers Grizzoli, Fangmeyer, Delgato: your teams take missing mammals from the Rainforest District. Officers McHorn, Rhinowitz, Wolfard: your teams take Sahara Square. Officers Higgins, Snarlov, Trunkaby: Tundratown. And finally, our first bunny, Officer Hopps."

Judy sat up, she'd been waiting anxiously for her assignment. Bogo grabbed the last case file from Higgins and held it dramatically in the air as he looked at Judy.

"Parking duty. Dismissed!"

"Parking duty?" asked Judy quietly. She hurried after Bogo. "Uh, Chief? Chief Bogo?"

Bogo looked around and saw no one until he

looked down to see Judy at his ankles.

"Sir, you said there are fourteen missing mammal cases."

"So?"

"So I can handle one. You probably forgot, but I was top of my class at the academy."

"Didn't forget. Just don't care."

"Sir, I'm not just some token bunny."

"Well, then writing a hundred tickets a day should be easy," said Bogo, walking out and slamming the door behind him.

"A hundred tickets," said Judy, stomping her foot. She turned toward the closed door and shouted, "I'm gonna write *two hundred* tickets! Before noon!"

Sporting her traffic-enforcement hat and a bright-orange vest, Judy climbed into her parking cart, buckled up, and put on her shades. She pressed the gas pedal down and took off . . . very slowly.

Judy's ears twisted and turned as she used her excellent hearing skills to listen for expired parking meters. Each time one dinged, she dashed over and wrote a ticket. She ticketed dozens of cars of every size—moose cars, mouse cars, and everything in between.

"Boom! Two hundred tickets before noon," she said proudly.

She turned to see her traffic cart parked at an expired meter. "Two hundred and *one*," she said with a self-satisfied smile as she wrote *herself* a ticket.

Then the sound of a car horn and an angry sheep yelling out his window interrupted her moment.

"Watch where you're going, fox!" the sheep yelled.

Judy saw a red fox across the street and eyed him suspiciously. Then she shook her head and scolded herself for being suspicious without a real reason. But when she saw him look around before slinking into Jumbeaux's Café, she crossed the road and peeked in through the window. He was nowhere to be seen.

Now completely suspicious, Judy unsnapped the pink can of fox repellent from her holster and headed inside.

The café was an elephant ice cream parlor. Elephants used their trunks to scoop ice cream into bowls and decorate sundaes with nuts, whipped cream, and cherries. Judy spotted the fox at the front of the line. Jerry Jumbeaux, Jr., the elephant working behind the counter, yelled at the fox. "Listen, I don't know what you're doing skulking around during daylight hours, but I don't want any trouble here. So hit the road!"

"I'm not looking for any trouble either, sir, I simply want to buy a Jumbo-pop," said the fox innocently, reaching behind him, "for my little boy. You want the red or the blue, pal?"

When Judy noticed the little toddler clinging to the fox's leg, she felt awful for jumping to conclusions. "I'm such a . . . ," Judy muttered to herself as she turned to leave.

"Listen, buddy. There aren't any fox ice cream joints in your part of town?"

"There are. It's just, my boy—" The fox tousled the boy's fur. "This goofy little stinker—he loves all things elephant. Wants to be one when he grows up. Who the heck am I to crush the little guy's dreams?"

The boy pulled up the hood of his elephant costume and made a cute little *toot-toot* sound with his toy elephant trunk. Judy smiled. Realizing she still had it out, she quickly tucked her fox repellent back into its holster.

"Look, you probably can't read, fox, but the sign says"—Jerry pointed to the sign as he read it slowly— "WE RESERVE THE RIGHT TO REFUSE SERVICE TO ANYONE. So beat it."

"You're holding up the line," said an annoyed elephant, waiting behind them.

The little toddler looked as if he was about to cry. Judy marched up to the counter and flashed her badge at Jerry.

"Hello? Excuse me?" said Judy.

"You're gonna have to wait your turn like everyone else, meter maid," said Jerry.

"Actually . . . I'm an officer. Just had a quick question. Are your customers aware that they're getting snot and mucous with their cookies and cream?"

"What are you talking about?" asked Jerry, annoyed.

"Well, I don't want to cause you any trouble, but I believe scooping ice cream with an ungloved trunk is a class-three health-code violation. Which is kind of a big deal. Of course, I could let you off with a warning if you were to glove those trunks and—I don't know—finish selling this nice dad and his son a . . . what was it?" Judy smiled at the fox.

"A Jumbo-pop," said the fox.

"A Jumbo-pop," said Judy firmly.

Jerry stared for a moment, then said, "Fifteen dollars."

The fox turned to Judy. "Thank you so much. Thank you." He dug through his pockets before stopping in disbelief. "Are you kidding me? I don't have my wallet. I'm sorry, pal, worst birthday ever." The fox leaned down to give the toddler a kiss, then turned to Judy. "Thanks anyway."

Judy slapped some cash on the counter. "Keep the change," she said.

Once Jerry gave them the Jumbo-pop, Judy held the door as the fox and his little boy exited Jumbeaux's.

"Officer, I can't thank you enough," said the fox. "So kind, really. Can I pay you back?"

"Oh no, my treat. It just—you know, it burns me up to see folks with such backward attitudes toward foxes," Judy said. "Well, I just wanna say, you're a great dad and just a . . . a real articulate fellow."

"Ah, well, that is high praise. It's rare that I find someone so non-patronizing . . . Officer . . ."

"Hopps. Mr. . . . ," Judy said, not catching the sarcasm that was evident in the fox's tone.

"Wilde. Nick Wilde."

Judy bent down toward the little fox. "And you, little guy, you want to be an elephant when you grow up . . . you be an elephant—because this is Zootopia, and anyone can be anything." She placed a ZPD badge sticker on the boy's chest.

"All right, here you go—" Nick said, handing him the huge Jumbo-pop. "Two paws. Yeah. Aw, look at that smile, that's a happy birthday smile! Give her a little bye-bye toot-toot."

The adorable little fox tooted his trunk.

"Toot-toot!" said Judy happily. Then she walked off with a spring in her step. It felt great to help somebody in need!

7

A little while later, Judy was writing parking tickets in Sahara Square when she noticed Nick and his kid a few blocks away. "Oh! Hey, little toot-toot!" she called, waving, but they didn't see her.

She started toward them but stopped suddenly when she realized what they were doing. They were *melting* the giant Jumbo-pop she had bought for them in the hot sun. Then they were channeling the juice into little jugs. Judy furrowed her brow as she watched Nick and his kid packing the full jugs into the back of a van. Her eyes nearly fell out of her head when she saw Nick's little son get into the driver's seat! Then they drove off. Judy was shocked and confused.

She hopped in her cart and followed them to the coldest section of Zootopia—Tundratown. Nick's son was using his little paws to make molds in the snow, which Nick then put sticks in. Then the two poured the juice from the melted Jumbo-pop into the molds to create dozens of smaller pops! Judy looked on, scandalized. She couldn't believe it!

Judy followed them again, this time to Savanna Central, where they set up a stand and sold "pawpsicles" at marked-up prices to lemmings.

"Pawpsicles! Get your pawpsicles!" barked Nick.

One lemming bought an icy treat, and then the rest of them followed. In an instant, the frozen desserts were completely sold out! Once the lemmings finished their pawpsicles, they threw the sticks into a recycling bin. When the lemmings were gone, a small door opened in the bin and the little fox—who, Judy realized, was *not* an adorable toddler but a *fully grown* fennec fox named Finnick—stepped out with a bundle of used pawpsicle sticks. Judy was having trouble believing her eyes.

She continued to follow Nick and Finnick to Little Rodentia, where Nick plopped down the bundle of used sticks in front of a mouse construction worker and shouted, "Lumber delivery!"

"What's with the color?" asked the construction worker.

"The color? It's *red* wood," answered Nick, shrugging off the question as he accepted his payment.

The construction workers hauled the sticks away, and Judy watched in awe as Nick handed Finnick his share of the cash.

"Thirty-nine . . . forty. There you go. Way to work that diaper, big guy. What, no kiss bye-bye for Daddy?" Nick asked jokingly.

"You kiss me tomorrow, I'll bite your face off," said Finnick in a deep voice. *"Ciao."* Finnick hopped into his van and drove off, blaring loud rap music.

Judy appeared in front of Nick, her face burning with anger. "I stood up for you. And you lied to me! You *liar*!" she yelled.

"It's called a hustle, sweetheart," said Nick coolly. "And I'm not the liar, he is." Nick pointed behind Judy. She turned but saw no one standing there. When she whipped back around, Nick was gone! Then she spotted his tail disappearing behind a corner.

"Hey," she said, hurrying to catch up as Nick strolled along. "All right, slick Nick, you're under arrest."

"Really, for what?"

"Gee, I don't know. How about selling food without a permit, transporting undeclared commerce across borough lines, false advertising—"

"Permit." Nick smiled as he showed Judy the

document. "Receipt of declared commerce." He showed her a receipt. "And I did not falsely advertise anything. Take care."

"You told that mouse the pawpsicle sticks were redwood," Judy said.

"That's right," said Nick smugly. "Red. Wood. With a space in the middle. Wood that is red. You can't touch me, Carrots. I've been doing this since I was born."

"You're gonna want to refrain from calling me Carrots."

"My bad," said Nick. "I just naturally assumed you came from some little carrot-choked Podunk, no?"

"Ah, no," Judy replied, as if to say "obviously not." "Podunk is in Deerbrooke County. I grew up in Bunnyburrow."

"Okay. Tell me if this story sounds familiar." Nick's tone changed as he began to talk quickly and boldly. "Naïve little hick with good grades and big ideas decides, 'Hey, look at me, I'm gonna move to Zootopia, where predators and prey live in harmony and sing "Kumbaya"!' Only to find—whoopsie, we don't all get along. And that dream of being a big-city cop? Double whoopsie! She's a meter maid. And whoopsie number threesie, *no one* cares about her or her dreams. Soon enough those dreams die and our bunny sinks into emotional and literal squalor, living in a box under a bridge. Until, finally, she has no choice but to go back home with that cute fuzzy wuzzy tail between her legs to become— You're from Bunnyburrow? So let's say a carrot farmer? Sound about right?"

Judy stood speechless. She couldn't believe Nick had figured out her fears so quickly. A passing rhino almost pushed her down, knocking her out of her thoughts.

"Be careful now," warned Nick. "Or it won't just be your dreams getting crushed."

"Hey, hey!" she said, trying to pull herself together. "No one tells me what I can or can't be! Especially not some jerk who never had the guts to try and be anything more than a pawpsicle hustler."

"All right, look, everyone comes to Zootopia thinking they can be anything they want. Well, you can't. You can only be what you are." He pointed to himself. "Sly fox." Then he pointed to her. "Dumb bunny."

"I am *not* a dumb bunny."

"Right. And that's not wet cement."

Judy looked down to see that she was ankle-deep

in gooey wet cement. She sighed in dismay.

"You'll never be a real cop," Nick said obnoxiously. "You're a cute meter maid, though. Maybe a supervisor one day. Hang in there."

Frustrated, Judy watched as Nick walked off. Then she set about pulling her paws out of the cement.

Shhhk! *Shhhk!* Judy dragged her cement-covered paws across the welcome mat outside her apartment before going in. A sad song filled the air when she turned on the radio. She switched stations. It was another sad song. And that was how her day was going. After listening to a few depressing songs, she dragged her feet over to the kitchen and popped in a Carrots for One microwave dinner.

Beep! Beep! Once it was done, she peeled open the cover, revealing a single shriveled carrot. With her ears drooping, Judy sat down at her small table and ate her dinner alone.

Brrring! Brrring! Judy's cell phone rang. It was her parents calling for a video chat. She shook her head, sighed, and forced a smile before answering. "Oh, hey! It's my parents . . . ," she said, trying to sound upbeat.

"There she is!" said Bonnie. "Hi, sweetheart!"

Stu's face popped onto the screen. "Hey there, Jude the Dude! How was your first day on the force?"

"It was real great," said Judy, knowing this was a complete lie.

"Yeah? Everything you ever hoped?" asked Bonnie.

"Absolutely, and more! Everyone's so nice. And I feel like I'm really making a difference—"

"Wait a second," said Stu, popping his head onto the screen again. "Holy cripes, Bonnie! Look at that!"

Bonnie peered into the screen trying to see what Stu was so excited about. "Oh my sweet heaven! Judy, are you a meter maid?"

Judy had forgotten she was still wearing her vest and that her hat was on the chair. She tried to backpedal. "What? Oh, this? No. It's just a temporary—"

"It's the safest job on the force!" exclaimed Bonnie happily.

"She's not a real cop! Our prayers have been answered!" said Stu, overjoyed.

"Glorious day!"

"Meter maid! Meter maid! Meter maid!" chanted Stu.

"Dad. Dad!" said Judy, feeling uncomfortable and just wanting to end the conversation. "You know what? This has been great, guys, but it's been a long day—"

"That's right. You get some rest!" said Bonnie.

"Absolutely. Those meters aren't gonna maid themselves," added Stu.

They said goodnight and Judy hung up, feeling even sadder than she had before. As she took off her vest, she turned on more sad music. Through the wall, Oryx yelled: "Hey, bunny! Turn down that depressing music!"

"Leave the meter maid alone!" yelled Kudu. "Didn't you hear her conversation? She feels like a failure!"

Judy turned down the music as Oryx and Kudu continued to yell and bicker.

"Tomorrow's another day," she said quietly to herself.

"Yeah, but it might be worse!" yelled Oryx.

Exhausted, Judy settled in for the night, wondering what tomorrow would bring.

9

The next day, Judy was back to ticketing cars parked at expired meters. She plunked a ticket down, and a moose yelled at her: "I was thirty seconds over!"

As another meter dinged, Judy scribbled the ticket and placed it on a tiny windshield.

"You're a real hero, lady!" yelled an angry mouse.

Ding! Judy wrote out a third ticket, which a hippo picked up. Her small child looked at Judy and said, "My mommy says she wishes you were dead."

An angry driver shouted, "Uncool, rabbit. My tax dollars pay your salary."

Later, Judy got into her cart and turned the key. But the engine wouldn't start. She banged her head against the steering wheel, making the horn honk.

"I am a real cop," she muttered weakly. "I am a real cop. I am a real cop. . . ."

"Hey hey!" called a frantic pig, running toward her.

The pig pounded on her cart window. "You! Bunny!"

"Sir, if you have a grievance, you may contest your citation in—" she responded mechanically.

"What're you talking about?" shouted the pig. "My shop! It just got robbed! Look, he's getting away! Well! Are you a cop or not?"

"Oh, yes," said Judy, snapping out of it. "Don't worry, sir. I got this!"

She spotted a weasel running down the street, carrying a bag of stolen goods and jumped out of her cart.

"Stop!" she yelled, chasing the thief. "Stop in the name of the law!"

"Catch me if you can, cottontail!" shouted the weasel.

McHorn screeched up in his patrol car. "This is Officer McHorn. We've got a 10-31," the rhinoceros said into his radio.

Judy slid right across McHorn's hood as she ripped off her vest and hat and shouted, "I got dibs! Officer Hopps. I am in pursuit!"

She chased the weasel through Savanna Central, dodging giant elephants along the way.

Then the weasel ducked into the tiny community of Little Rodentia. The large cops, who had joined in the chase, couldn't fit through the gate, but Judy was small enough to follow the weasel in.

"You!" she yelled forcefully. "Freeze!"

"Hey, meter maid! Wait for the real cops!" called McHorn.

Little Rodentia was packed with tiny rodents, and Judy and the weasel looked like giants pounding down its small streets.

A mouse school bus swerved to avoid the weasel and flew skyward. Judy caught it in midair, preventing a disaster. The mice inside cheered as she gently placed the bus on the ground. Judy watched the weasel jump off the top of a mouse building, tipping it over. She struggled to protect each and every building the weasel knocked into. Then he leapt on top of a moving mouse train!

"Bon voyage, flatfoot!" said the weasel with a chuckle, riding the train away.

But Judy wasn't about to give up. She ran even faster, until she was able to push him off the train. Rodents screamed and ran as Judy and the weasel came barreling through their midst.

"Hey!" she yelled. "Stop right there!"

"Have a donut, copper!" the weasel said with a laugh as he yanked a huge donut sign from the front of a shop. He flung it at Judy, but it missed and bounced toward some shrews coming out of Mousy's department store.

"Ohmygawd, did you see those leopard-print jeggings?" said a fashionable shrew to her friends. She turned to see the donut bouncing toward her and screamed in terror. *"Aaaaaaaaaaagh!"*

A second before it crushed the shrew, Judy moved in front of the donut and caught it in her arms. Then she turned to the shrew and said, "I love your hair."

"Awww . . . thank you," said the shrew gratefully.

Out of the corner of her eye, Judy noticed that the weasel was about to get away. She threw the giant donut over his head and around his body, trapping him inside. The weasel was stuck!

It wasn't long before the weasel, still inside the donut, rolled through the front door of the ZPD lobby and hit Clawhauser's desk.

"I popped the weasel!" Judy exclaimed.

Chief Bogo yelled from the other room: "HOPPS!"

Like a kid in the principal's office, Judy sat on a giant chair in front of Chief Bogo as he reviewed the report in front of him.

"Abandoning your post, inciting a scurry, reckless endangerment of rodents . . . but to be fair, you did

39

stop a master criminal from stealing two dozen . . . um, let's see . . . moldy onions." Bogo looked straight at the bag on his desk that Judy had confiscated from the crook she had stopped—Duke Weaselton.

"Hate to disagree with you, sir, but those aren't onions," Judy replied. "Those are a crocus varietal called *Midnicampum holicithias*. They're a class C botanical, sir. I grew up in a family where plant husbandry was kind of a *thing*."

"Shut your tiny mouth, now," said Bogo.

"Sir, I got the bad guy. That's my job."

"Your job is putting tickets on parked cars."

Bogo's intercom clicked as Clawhauser's voice came through. "Chief, uh, Mrs. Otterton's here to see you again."

"Not now," answered Bogo.

"Okay, I just didn't know if you wanted to take it this time—" said Clawhauser.

"Not now!"

Judy said, "Sir, I don't want to be a meter maid. I want to be a—"

"Do you think the mayor asked what I wanted before he assigned you to me?" Bogo interrupted her.

"But, sir—"

"Life isn't some cartoon musical where you sing a

little song and your insipid dreams magically come true. So let it go."

Just then a female otter, Mrs. Otterton, barged in with Clawhauser trailing behind, wheezing.

"Chief Bogo, please, just five minutes of your time," pleaded Mrs. Otterton.

"I'm sorry, sir, I tried to stop her; she is super slippery. I gotta go sit down," said Clawhauser, panting.

"Ma'am, as I've told you, we are doing everything we can," said Bogo.

"My husband has been missing for ten days," said Mrs. Otterton. "His name is Emmitt Otterton." She held up a family photo.

"Yes, I know," said Bogo.

"He's a florist," she added. "We have two beautiful children. He would never just disappear."

"Ma'am, our detectives are very busy."

"Please. There's got to be somebody to find my Emmitt."

Bogo tried to calm Mrs. Otterton down, but nothing worked. She kept going on about her concern over Mr. Otterton's disappearance.

"I will find him," said Judy.

Bogo looked at Judy as if he was about to explode. He watched as Mrs. Otterton hugged Judy tightly.

"Bless you, bless you, little bunny!" she said, relieved. "You find my Emmitt and bring him home to me and my babies, please."

Bogo grunted and ushered Mrs. Otterton back outside. "Mrs. Otterton? Please wait out here."

Bogo closed the door and turned to Judy, furious. "You're fired."

"What? Why?" she asked.

"Insubordination. Now, I'm going to open this door, and you are going to tell that otter you're a former meter maid with delusions of grandeur who will not be taking the case."

Bogo opened the door and there was Assistant Mayor Bellwether, hugging Mrs. Otterton.

"I just heard Officer Hopps is taking the case!" said Bellwether happily. Bellwether pulled out her phone and began texting. "The Mammal Inclusion Initiative is really paying off! Mayor Lionheart is just going to be so jazzed!"

"Let's not tell the mayor just yet—" said Bogo.

"And I sent it, and it's done, so I did do that," interrupted Bellwether. "Well, I'd say the case is in good hands!" Bellwether smiled at Judy. "Us little guys really need to stick together! Right?"

"Like glue!" Judy responded.

"Good one," Bellwether said. "Just call me if you ever need anything. You've always got a friend at city hall, Judy. All right, bye bye!"

"Thank you, ma'am," Judy said.

Bogo forced a smile and closed the door. He turned to Judy, even angrier than before. "I will give you forty-eight hours," he said.

"YES!" cried Judy.

"That's two days to find Emmitt Otterton."

"Okay."

"But you strike out, you resign."

Judy couldn't believe what he was suggesting. "Oh, uh . . ." She thought for a moment and then nodded. "Okay . . . deal," she said.

"Splendid. Clawhauser will give you the complete case file," Bogo said.

Excited, Judy rushed out to the front desk to retrieve the case file. "Here you go!" sang Clawhauser, handing her the file. "One missing otter!"

Judy opened the folder and her jaw dropped. Inside was a single piece of paper. "That's it?" she said in disbelief.

"Yikes! That is the smallest case file I've ever seen! Leads: none. Witnesses: none. And you're not in the computer system yet, so resources: none." Clawhauser chuckled. "I hope you didn't stake your career on cracking this one," he said, smiling.

Judy didn't smile back. Clawhauser took a bite of his donut and crumbs landed on the picture inside the file.

"Last known sighting . . . ," she said, looking at the photo under Clawhauser's donut crumbs. The picture was from a traffic camera and showed Mr. Otterton on the street. Judy blew the crumbs off and noticed something about the picture. She squinted. Still unable to see, she looked around. "Let me borrow that." She grabbed Clawhauser's empty soda bottle. She looked through it, using the glass at the bottom to magnify the image. Now she could see Mr. Otterton holding a frozen treat. She examined it and said thoughtfully, "Pawpsicle."

"The murder weapon!" Clawhauser said, nodding.

"Get your pawpsicle . . . ," Judy said, thinking back to the incident with Nick.

"Yeah, because . . . What does that mean?" asked Clawhauser.

"It means I . . . have a *lead*." She headed out, leaving Clawhauser sitting at his desk, confused.

Judy drove around in her traffic cart until she found Nick pushing a baby stroller down the street. She smiled when she saw him. "Hi! Hello? It's me again!"

"Hey, it's Officer Toot-Toot," said Nick with a smirk.

"Ha-ha-ho!" Judy gave a fake laugh, humoring him. "No, actually, it's Officer Hopps, and I'm here to ask you some questions about a case."

"What happened, meter maid?" asked Nick. "Did someone steal a traffic cone? It wasn't me."

Nick walked on, pushing the stroller around the corner. Judy pulled in front of him.

"Carrots, you're gonna wake the baby. I've got to get to work," said Nick.

"This is important, sir. I think your ten dollars' worth of pawpsicles can wait."

Nick faced her and raised his eyebrows. "I make

two hundred bucks a day, Fluff. Three hundred sixty-five days a year, since I was twelve. And time is money, so hop along."

"Please, just look at the picture," said Judy, holding up the picture of Mr. Otterton. "You sold Mr. Otterton that pawpsicle, right? Do you know him?"

"Lady, I know everybody. I also know that somewhere there's a toy store missing its stuffed animals, so why don't you get back to your box?"

Judy's ears drooped. "Fine," she said. "Then we'll have to do this the hard way." She slapped a parking boot onto the wheel of the stroller, locking it in place.

"Did you just boot my stroller?"

"Nicholas Wilde, you are under arrest," Judy said.

Nick smiled, amused. "For what?

"Felony tax evasion," she replied.

Nick's smile quickly dropped.

"Yeah . . . ," continued Judy. "Two hundred dollars a day . . . three hundred sixty-five days a year . . . since you were twelve. That's two decades, so times twenty . . . which is one million, four hundred sixty thousand—I think, I mean I am just a dumb bunny—but we are good at multiplying. Anyway, according to your tax forms"—Judy presented some tax forms to Nick—"you reported, let me see here, zero. Unfortunately, lying on a federal form is a punishable offense. Five years jail time."

"Well, it's my word against yours," said Nick.

Judy held up a carrot-shaped pen and clicked a button. Suddenly, a recording of Nick's voice played from a speaker inside the pen: "I make two hundred bucks a day, Fluff. Three hundred sixty-five days a year, since I was twelve."

"Actually, it's your word against yours," Judy said. "And if you want this pen, you're going to cooperate with my investigation or the only place you'll be selling pawpsicles is the prison cafeteria." She grinned. "It's called a hustle, sweetheart."

From the baby stroller, Finnick laughed hysterically. "She hustled you. She hustled you good. You're a cop now, Nick; you're gonna need one of these!" Finnick slapped his ZPD badge sticker on Nick. "Have fun working with the fuzz!" Finnick jumped out of his stroller and walked away.

Nick took the photo of Mr. Otterton and looked at it.

"Start talking," said Judy.

"I don't know where he is. I only saw where he went."

Judy smiled broadly at him and patted the passenger

seat of her cart. "Great, let's go."

"It's not exactly a place for a cute little bunny," said Nick.

"Don't call me cute," Judy said. "Get in the car."

"Okay. You're the boss." Nick climbed in, and they headed off.

11

Nick led Judy to a place called the Mystic Spring Oasis. The scent of incense wafted through the air inside the gates, and a yak named Yax sat in meditation. Flies buzzed around his unshowered body. "Ooooooohmmmmm," he chanted. The tone of the buzzing flies seemed to match the tone of his voice. "Ooooooohmmmmm."

Judy approached Yax. "Hello! My name is—"

"Oh, you know, I'm gonna hit the pause button right there. We are all good on Bunny Scout Cookies," said Yax, who talked slowly, almost as if he wasn't quite there.

"I am Officer Hopps, ZPD. I am looking for a missing mammal, Emmitt Otterton"—she showed him the picture—"who may have frequented this establishment."

Yax looked at the photo and his eyes widened, as if

he was about to say something important.

"AH-CHOO!" he sneezed, and flies scattered everywhere before returning to their place, hovering around him. "Yep, Ol' Emmitt. Haven't seen him in a couple weeks. But hey, you should talk to his yoga instructor. I'd be happy to take you back." Yax nodded toward a different area of the club.

"Thank you so much," said Judy. "That would be a big—" Yax came around from behind the counter, and Judy was unable to complete her sentence when she saw what he was—or wasn't—wearing. "You are naked!"

"Huh? Oh, for sure, we're a Naturalist Club," said Yax nonchalantly.

"Yeah, in Zootopia anyone can be anything . . . ," said Nick, grinning, "and these guys, they be naked."

"Nanga's on the other side of the pleasure pool," offered Yax. "Right this way, folks."

Judy's jaw dropped as she wondered what a pleasure pool was. When they got there, naked animals were sunning themselves, playing, and lounging around. Judy's eyes nearly popped out of her head at the sight. Nick leaned over to her. "Does this make you uncomfortable? Because there is no shame in calling it quits. We could end our deal right now."

"Yes, there is," she said. She was determined more than ever to stay on the case.

"Boy, that's the spirit," joked Nick.

Out in the courtyard, Judy tried to act normal. Her eyes darted around, looking for a neutral place to land.

"Yeah, some mammals say the naturalist life is weird," said Yax. "But you know what I say is weird? Clothes on animals! Here we go. As you can see, Nanga's an elephant, so she'll totally remember everything."

Nanga looked curiously at the newcomers.

"Hey, Nanga, these dudes have some questions about Emmitt the otter," said Yax.

"Who?" Nanga asked.

"Emmitt Otterton," Yax prompted. "Been coming to your yoga class for like six years."

"I have no memory of this beaver," Nanga stated.

"Yeah, he's an otter, actually," Judy corrected, looking over at Nick in dismay.

"He was here a couple Wednesdays ago. 'Member?" Yax prompted Nanga.

But the elephant just shook her head. "Nope."

"Yeah," Yax continued. "He was wearing a green cable-knit sweater-vest and a new pair of corduroy slacks. Oh, and a paisley tie, sweet Windsor knot, real tight. Remember that, Nanga?"

Judy couldn't believe her luck. Yax was a gold mine! She scrambled to write everything down.

"No," Nanga said again.

"Uh, ah, you didn't happen to catch the license plate number did you?" Judy asked.

"Oh, for sure," Yax nodded. "It was 29THD03."

Judy's pen moved quickly. "—03. Wow. This is a lot of great info. Thank you."

Yax smiled. "Told ya Nanga had a mind like a steel trap. I wish I had a memory like an elephant."

Outside the club, in Sahara Square, Nick smiled smugly. "Well, I had a ball. You are welcome for the clue. And seeing as how any moron can run a plate, I'll take that pen and bid you adieu."

Judy held out the pen, but as Nick went to reach for it, she realized something. She pulled it back before he could swipe it. "The plate . . . I can't run the plate. . . . I'm not in the system yet." She put the pen back in her pocket and smiled at Nick.

"Gimme the pen, please," said Nick.

"What was it you said? 'Any moron can run a plate'? Gosh . . . if only there were a moron around who was up to the task . . . ," she said.

"Rabbit, I did what you asked; you can't keep me on the hook forever," said Nick.

"No, not forever. I have"—Judy paused as she checked her phone—"thirty-six hours left to solve this case. Can you run the plate or not?"

Nick stared at Judy, and then slowly grinned. "I just remembered, I have a pal at the DMV."

12

Inside the Department of Mammal Vehicles, there was a huge line of animals waiting to be helped.

"They're all sloths!" Judy exclaimed, noticing the employees. Nick smiled. "You said this was going to be quick!"

"What? Are you saying that because he's a sloth, he can't be fast?" Nick said innocently. "I thought in Zootopia anyone could be anything."

Nick led Judy over to his friend, Flash, who was sitting behind the counter at one of the windows. "Flash, Flash, hundred-yard dash!" said Nick. "Buddy, it's nice to see ya."

Flash looked at Nick for a long beat. "Nice to . . . see you . . . too," he said slowly.

"Flash, I'd love you to meet my friend. Darling, I seem to have forgotten your name."

"Officer Judy Hopps," said Judy, showing her

badge. "ZPD. How are you?"

Flash looked at her and didn't respond for a good ten seconds. "I am . . . doing . . . just—"

Judy couldn't take it. "Fine?" she offered, trying to move the conversation along.

". . . as well . . . as . . . I can . . . be. What—" Flash continued.

"Hang in there," said Nick, loving every second.

". . . can I . . . do . . ."

"Well, I was hoping you could run a plate—"

". . . for you . . ."

"Well, I was hoping you could—"

". . . today?" Flash asked, finally completing his sentence.

"Well, I was hoping you could run a plate for us. We're in a really big hurry," answered Judy.

Flash waited a moment before beginning his response. "Sure. What's the . . . plate—"

"Two nine—" Judy began.

". . . number?" asked Flash.

Judy took a deep breath. "29THD03."

Flash took another moment before repeating it. "Two . . . nine . . ."

"THD03," said Judy.

"T," said Flash.

It took quite a while for Flash to enter the first part of the license plate number into the system. Just as he was about to punch in the last digit, Nick interrupted him. "Hey, Flash, you wanna hear a joke?"

"No!" Judy yelled.

"What do you call a three-humped camel?"

"I don't . . . know. What do . . . you call . . . a—"

"Three-humped camel," said Judy quickly, trying to get the joke out of the way.

". . . three-humped . . . camel?" said Flash.

"Pregnant," answered Nick.

Flash showed no reaction at first, but then he slowly raised his head as a smile crept across his face. "Ha . . . ha . . . ha . . . ha . . ."

Judy's impatience grew. "Ha, ha, yes, very funny, very funny. Can we please just focus on the—"

Flash turned toward the sloth next to him. "Hey, Priscilla . . ."

"Yes . . . Flash?" answered Priscilla, just as slowly.

"What . . . do . . . you call . . . a—"

"A three-humped camel? Pregnant!" shouted Judy, thoroughly frustrated.

"Three . . . humped . . ."

Judy was losing her mind. *"Aaaaaaaaaagh!"*

Hours after they'd entered, a dot-matrix printer slowly spat out the address for the license plate number.

"Here you . . . ," said Flash, handing it to Judy.

"Yeah, yeah, yeah . . . thank you!" she said.

". . . go."

"29THD03," said Judy, frantically reading the printout. "It's registered to . . . Tundratown Limo-Service? A limo took Otterton, and the limo's in Tundratown— It's in Tundratown!"

"Way to hustle, buddy," Nick said to Flash. "I love you. I owe you."

"Hurry, we gotta beat the rush hour and—" Judy said as she hurried through the door to get outside. "IT'S NIGHT!" She looked at the sky in awe. It was completely dark.

They had been in there for hours! Judy was running out of time.

13

Judy and Nick drove to frigid Tundratown, where everything was covered in snow and ice. When they found Tundratown Limo-Service, it was locked up tight.

"Closed," Judy said, gesturing to the lock on the gate. "Great."

"And I will bet you don't have a warrant to get in. Hmm? Darn it. It's a bummer," said Nick.

"You wasted the day on purpose," said Judy.

"Madam, I have a fake badge. I would never impede your pretend investigation."

"It is not a pretend investigation!" Judy said, showing Nick the picture of Otterton. "Look! See! See him? This otter is missing!"

"Well, then they should have gotten a real cop to find him."

She wasn't going to let Nick get to her. "What

is your problem?" she asked. "Does seeing me fail somehow make you feel better about your own sad, miserable life?"

Nick appeared to consider her question before answering. "It does. One hundred percent. Now . . . since you're sans warrant, I guess we're done?"

Judy sighed, defeated. "Fine," she said. "We are done. Here's your pen." She threw the pen over the fence, into the lot.

"Hey," said Nick, staring at her, puzzled. "First off, you throw like a bunny, and second, you are a very sore loser." Nick started to climb over the fence. "See you later, Officer Fluff. So sad this is over. Wish I could've helped more—"

Nick jumped down to the other side of the fence and reached for the pen, but Judy was already there, beating him to it.

"The thing is, " Judy said, "you don't need a warrant if you have probable cause. And I'm pretty sure I saw a shifty lowlife climbing the fence, so you're helping plenty. Come on," she said, heading off as she whistled a merry tune.

Nick watched her, annoyed, but his face also showed a morsel of respect for her trick.

In the parking lot, Nick wiped snow off the back of a bumper to show the plate.

"29THD03," read Judy. "This is it."

The limousine was actually a "refrigousine." It had a heavy refrigerator door and was cold inside. Judy pulled out an evidence bag with tweezers as she and Nick snooped around the chilly limo.

"Polar bear fur," she said, holding up a piece of fur trapped in her tweezers.

"OH MY GOD!" said Nick.

"What? What!" exclaimed Judy, whirling to see the source of Nick's excitement. He had opened the glove compartment.

"*The Velvety Pipes of Jerry Vole!*" said Nick, showing her CDs. "But on CD? Who still uses CDs?"

Judy rolled her eyes and went back to collecting real clues. Nick lowered the back partition, and his eyebrows shot up. "Carrots, if your otter was here . . . he had a very bad day."

Nick and Judy stared at the backseat. It had been shredded! Violent-looking claw marks were scraped across it.

"You ever seen anything like this?" asked Judy.

Nick shook his head, actually concerned. "No."

Judy spotted a wallet on the floor and picked it up. She opened it to find Mr. Otterton's driver's license and business cards for his floral shop. "This is him! Emmitt Otterton. He was definitely here. What do you think happened?"

Nick shook his head, stumped. Then his eyes drifted to the cocktail glasses at the bar inside the limo. They were etched with the letter *B*.

"Wait a minute," said Nick suspiciously. "Polar bear fur . . . Rat Pack music . . . fancy cups . . ." He turned to Judy. "I know whose car this is. We gotta go."

"Why? Whose car is it?" she asked.

Nick rushed around the limo, nervously trying to put everything back the way they found it. "The most dangerous crime boss in Tundratown. They call him Mr. Big, and *he* does *not* like me, so we've gotta go!"

"I'm not leaving," said Judy. "This is a crime scene."

"Well, it's gonna be an even bigger crime scene if Mr. Big finds me, so we are leaving right now!"

Nick made a break for the limo door, but when he opened it, two big polar bears looked down at him. "Raymond! And is that Kevin?" said Nick, trying to

sound excited. "Long time no see! And speaking of no see, how about you forget you saw me? For old times' sake?"

Without saying a word, the polar bears yanked Nick and Judy out of the limo. They shoved them into a car and sandwiched Nick and Judy between them.

"What did you do to make Mr. Big so mad at you?" Judy asked Nick.

"I, uh, may or may not have sold him a very expensive wool rug . . . that was made from the fur of a . . . skunk's butt," Nick said quietly.

"Sweet cheese and crackers," said Judy.

A short time later, the car pulled through a guarded security gate into a giant residential compound that was the home of Mr. Big.

14

Judy and Nick were led inside the house and into a lavishly decorated office. A large polar bear entered the room.

"Is that Mr. Big?" Judy whispered to Nick.

"No," he answered.

An even bigger polar bear lumbered in behind. "What about him? Is that him?" Judy asked.

"No," said Nick, frustrated.

An even bigger polar bear showed up, following the others. "Okay, that's gotta be him," Judy said.

"Stop talking, stop talking, stop talking—"

The largest polar bear held a teeny tiny chair in his giant paw. Sitting on the chair was a little Arctic shrew.

"Mr. Big, sir, this is a simple misunder—" Nick started.

Judy stared at the tiny shrew in wide-eyed surprise. *He* was Mr. Big?

Mr. Big held out his tiny finger, and Nick kissed the ring wrapped around it.

"This is a simple misunderstanding," said Nick.

Mr. Big motioned for Nick to be quiet. "You come here unannounced . . . on the day my daughter is to be married?" Mr. Big's raspy voice had an authoritative tone to it, but it also sounded like his body: very tiny.

"Well, actually, we were brought here against our will, so. . . . Point is, I did not know it was your car, and I certainly did not know about your daughter's wedding," Nick said, chuckling nervously.

"I trusted you, Nicky. I welcomed you into my home. We broke bread together. Gram-mama made you her cannoli." Mr. Big frowned and scratched his chin as he looked at Nick with cold eyes. "And how did you repay my generosity? With a rug . . . made from the butt of a skunk. A skunk-butt rug. You disrespected me. You disrespected my gram-mama, who I buried in that skunk-butt rug. I told you never to show your face here again, but here you are, snooping around with this . . ." Mr. Big gestured to Judy. "What are you, a performer? What's with the costume?"

Judy tried to answer. "Sir, I am a co—"

"Mime!" Nick shouted, cutting her off. "She is a

mime. This mime cannot speak. You can't speak if you're a mime."

"No," said Judy. "I am a cop."

Mr. Big shifted in his tiny chair, agitated.

"And I'm on the Emmitt Otterton case. My evidence puts him in your car, so intimidate me all you want; I'm going to find out what you did to that otter if it's the last thing I do."

Mr. Big considered Judy and grunted. "Then I have only one request: say hello to Gram-mama. Ice 'em!" he shouted to the polar bears.

"Whoa! I didn't see nothing! I'm not saying nothing!" Nick said, trying to squirm his way out of death by ice.

"And you never will," said Mr. Big coolly.

The polar bears picked Judy and Nick up, ready to throw them down into a freezing pit of ice and water the bears had opened in front of Mr. Big's desk.

"Please!" Nick begged. "No, no, no! If you're mad at me about the rug, I've got more rugs!"

The polar bears held Nick and Judy over the pit. Then Mr. Big's daughter, Fru Fru, who was as tiny as her father, entered, wearing a wedding gown.

"Oh, Daddy, it's time for our dance," she said. She noticed Judy and Nick and sighed, clearly annoyed.

"What did we say? No icing anyone at my wedding."

"I have to, baby," said Mr. Big. "Daddy has to." Then he turned to Nick and Judy and calmly said, "Ice 'em."

Nick and Judy screamed.

"Wait. WAIT!" Fru Fru shouted. "I know her. She's the bunny who saved my life yesterday. From that giant donut."

It was the stylish shrew from Little Rodentia.

"This bunny?" asked Mr. Big.

"Yes!" She turned to Judy. "Hi," she said sweetly.

"Hi," said Judy. "I love your dress."

"Aw, thank you," said Fru Fru.

Mr. Big motioned to the polar bears. "Put 'em down." Then he turned to Judy. "You have done me a great service. I will help you find the otter. I will take your kindness . . . and pay it forward."

Nick stood there, dumbfounded . . . and extremely happy not to be in a pit of ice.

15

Arctic animals danced as Fru Fru and her groom fed each other cake. Nick and Judy looked like giants as they sat at the head table, next to Mr. Big.

"Otterton is my florist," said Mr. Big. "He's like a part of the family. He had something important he wanted to discuss. That's why I sent that car to pick him up. But he never arrived."

"Because he was attacked," said Judy.

"No . . . *he* attacked," Mr. Big explained. "He went crazy. Ripped up the car, scared my driver half to death, and disappeared into the night."

"He's a sweet little otter," said Judy.

"My child, we may be evolved . . . but deep down, we are still animals."

Nick and Judy exchanged a worried look.

"You want to find Otterton . . . talk to the driver of the car. His name is Manchas, lives in the Rainforest

District. Only he can tell you more."

Judy and Nick left the wedding and headed straight for the lush, humid Rainforest District in search of their next clue.

As the steam trees pumped a steady stream of mist into the rainforest air, Judy and Nick climbed higher and higher. They followed a winding road to a home high up in the canopy. Once the steamy fog cleared, they could see Manchas's moss-covered apartment.

"Mr. Manchas?" Judy called, after ringing the doorbell. "Judy Hopps, ZPD. I'd like to ask you some questions about Emmitt Otterton." She knocked on the door as Nick snooped through Manchas's mailbox.

"He's a kitty," said Nick, holding up an issue of *Cat Fancy* magazine. "Hey, buddy, I got a can of tuna out here. Open the door, we'll talk it out—"

"Not every cat likes tuna," said Judy.

"Oh, right, got it," said Nick. He turned back to the door. "Buddy, I got a ball of yarn out here—"

Judy playfully punched Nick. "Sir, my partner's an

idiot. You're not in trouble. We just want to know what happened to Emmitt Otterton."

Finally, the door slowly creaked open, just a crack. "You should be asking . . . what happened to *me*," said a voice from inside.

The chain lock prevented the door from opening all the way. Through the space, they could see that Manchas was a big jaguar and he had been badly beaten, with bruises, scratches, and a black eye.

"Whoa. A teensy otter . . . did that?" asked Nick.

"What . . . happened?" Judy asked.

Manchas described the scene, sounding haunted. Like he was reliving it. "He was an *animal*, down on all fours. He was a savage. There was no warning, just kept yelling about 'the night howlers, the night howlers,' over and over."

Nick and Judy shared a look. "Oh. Wow. That's crazy, because that is actually why we came to talk to you . . . about the night howlers. Right?" said Judy, pumping for more information.

"Yes," said Nick, picking up on Judy's cue. "Absolutely. Whole ride over here we're sitting there going, *night howler* this, *night howler* that. Tell him."

"Yup. So you just open the door and tell us what you know, and we will tell you what we know," Judy persuaded. "Okay?"

Manchas considered a moment and then shut the door.

As he unlocked each of the locks from inside, Nick glanced at Judy, impressed. "You're not as dumb as you look," he said.

With a smile, she punched him on the arm. Hard.

They heard Manchas make a strange grunting noise.

"Mr. Manchas?" said Judy. "Are you okay?"

A loud thud sounded. Then the door creaked and opened just an inch. Judy slowly pushed it and saw Manchas hunched over in the middle of the room.

"Buddy?" Nick asked.

With a low growl, Manchas turned to them. His eyes were huge. He was SAVAGE! He raced at Nick and Judy like a primal predator.

"Run. *RUN!*" Judy screamed.

16

Nick and Judy ran for their lives as Manchas chased them.

"What is wrong with him?" shouted Nick.

"I don't know!"

They ran across a slippery suspension bridge with Manchas close behind. Nick stopped. "We're not gonna make it!"

"Jump!" Judy yelled.

They leapt off the bridge and landed on a low branch. Then they ducked into a hollow log, trying to hide, but Manchas continued to stalk them. Judy frantically picked up her police radio. "Officer Hopps to dispatch! Clawhauser, can you hear me?"

Inside the police station, Clawhauser was casually chatting with a coworker as he showed him a video on his phone.

"Have you seen Gazelle's new video—are you

familiar with Gazelle?" Clawhauser asked the coworker, not seeing the red light blinking on his phone. "Greatest singer of our lifetime—angel with horns. Yeah, you gotta check it out. So good. Do you see who's beside her right now?" He pointed to the screen, where he was dancing on a stage with Gazelle.

"Wow. You are one hot dancer," Gazelle's voice started, finishing with a robotic-type voice, "Benjamin Clawhauser."

"It's me!" Clawhauser exclaimed. "Did you think it was real? It looks so real! It's not—it's just a new app." He chuckled. Then he finally noticed his phone and clicked the speaker button. "Hold on—"

"Clawhauser!" Judy's voice rang out. Manchas, trying to get inside the log, took a swipe at her. "We have a 10-91! Jaguar gone savage! Vine and Tu-junga!"

"It's Tu-HUN-ga!" shouted Nick.

Manchas took another swipe at Judy, this time ripping her radio out of her hands. Nick and Judy scrambled out of the log and continued to run.

"Sending back up! Hopps? HOPPS?!" said Clawhauser, hearing the racket on the other end.

Nick and Judy spotted a gondola station. "There!" Judy yelled. "Head to the skytrams!"

They ran toward the gondolas. Judy darted out of

Manchas's way but slipped and got separated from Nick.

"Get in! Carrots? Carrots!" Nick called, trying to hold on to the gondola. But it pulled away.

"Go!" shouted Judy, struggling to regain her footing on the wet, slippery surface of the bridge.

Nick backed up and Manchas moved toward him, as if stalking his prey. "Buddy, one predator to another, if I offended you with the tuna thing, I meant no disrespe—"

Nick screamed as Manchas charged at him full speed. A split second before he reached Nick—*clank!* Manchas was yanked back by a handcuff on his back paw. Judy had cuffed him to a metal post! Nick couldn't believe it—Judy had saved his life.

"I can tell you're tense, so I'm just gonna give you a little personal space," Nick said to Manchas.

Manchas struggled angrily, knocking Nick and Judy over the edge of the walkway. Judy grabbed on to a vine with one arm and struggled to hold Nick with her other. As the two dangled over the canopy, Nick looked at the bottomless abyss below. Judy's mind raced as she tried to figure out what to do next.

"Rabbit, whatever you do, do not let go!" shouted Nick.

"I'm gonna let go!" said Judy.

"No . . . you what? You must have misunderstood me. I said don't—"

"One, two," Judy said, counting off as she started them swinging.

"RABBIT!"

She let go and swung them over to a net made of vines. It supported their weight for a moment. But then—*snap!* The vines broke and they plummeted toward the ground! Luckily, a cluster of vines had gotten tangled around their legs and stopped them right before they hit the rainforest floor.

Sirens rang out as a convoy of police cars screeched to a halt. Out of one stepped Chief Bogo. Judy smiled. The cavalry had arrived!

"Well, this should be good," said Bogo as he stared at Judy and Nick, who hung upside down, suspended from vines, in front of him.

17

Judy confidently led the cops up to the canopy. "I thought this was just a missing mammal case, but it's way bigger. Mr. Otterton did not just disappear. I believe he and this jaguar . . . they went savage, sir."

Bogo scoffed. "Savage? This isn't the Stone Age, Hopps. Animals don't go savage."

"I thought so, too, until I saw this." Judy turned the corner where she had handcuffed Manchas—but he was gone! Even the handcuffs had vanished.

"He was right here," she said, confused.

"The 'savage' jaguar," said Bogo, scoffing once again.

"Sir, I know what I saw. He almost killed us," said Judy.

"Or maybe an aggressive predator looks savage to you rabbits," Bogo said. He called out to the other officers, "Let's go."

"Wait—sir, I'm not the only one who saw him!"

Judy called to Nick, but before he could explain, Bogo said, "You think I'm going to believe a fox?"

"Well, he was a key witness, and I enlisted his services," Judy said.

Bogo shook his head, annoyed. "Two days to find the otter . . . or you quit . . . that was the deal. Badge," he said, waiting for her to hand her badge over.

Nick watched Judy stare at Bogo's outstretched hand. "Sir, we . . ."

"*Badge,*" said Bogo firmly.

Judy slowly reached for it as Nick spoke up. "Uh, no," he said.

Bogo glared at Nick. "What did you say, fox?"

"Sorry, what I said was 'no.' She will not be giving you that badge," said Nick. "Look, you gave her a clown vest and a three-wheel joke-mobile and two days to solve a case you guys haven't cracked in two weeks? Yeah, no wonder she needed to get help from a fox. None of you guys were gonna help her, were you?"

Judy stared at Nick. She couldn't believe he was sticking up for her. Bogo stood silently.

"Here's the thing, Chief. You gave her forty-eight hours, so technically we still have ten left to find our Mr. Otterton . . . and that's exactly what we are gonna do. So if you'll excuse us . . . we have a very big lead to follow and a case to crack. Good day."

Nick turned to Judy. "Officer Hopps?" He guided her to a passing gondola, leaving Bogo and the rest of the officers stunned.

"Thank you," she said as the two sat in the gondola while it soared over the Rainforest District.

"Never let them see that they get to you," said Nick.

Surprised, Judy turned to Nick. "So things get to you?"

"No . . . I mean, not anymore," said Nick. "But I was small and emotionally unbalanced like you once."

"Har-har," said Judy.

"No, it's true. I think I was eight, maybe nine, and all I wanted to do was join the Junior Ranger Scouts."

Nick decided to tell Judy a story about when he was a kid. "So my mom scraped together enough money to buy me a brand-new uniform." Nick explained how badly he wanted to fit in—even though he was the only predator in the troop. "I was gonna be part of a pack," he said.

Nick described the scene. He was taking the oath with the scouts when the other kids suddenly tackled him, yelling, "Get him! Get that pred! Muzzle him!"

They strapped a muzzle onto his snout and continued to mock him. "If you thought we'd ever trust a fox without a muzzle, you're even dumber than you look," one of them had taunted.

When they finally let him go, he ran away, limping, with his uniform torn to pieces.

"I learned two things that day," said Nick, lost in the terrible memory. "One, I was never going to let anyone see that they got to me."

"And two?" Judy prodded.

"If the world's only gonna see a fox as shifty and untrustworthy, there's no point trying to be anything else."

"Nick," said Judy gently. "You are so much more than that." She touched his arm as the gondola pierced through the clouds. They gazed down at the busy city buzzing below.

"Boy, look at that traffic down there," said Nick, changing the subject. "How about we go to Chuck in Traffic Central," Nick continued, pretending to be a cheesy radio announcer. "Chuck, how are things looking on those Jam Cams?"

"Nick, I'm glad you told me," said Judy.

"Wait! The Jam Cams!" said Nick urgently.

"Seriously, it's okay," said Judy.

"N-no, shh-shush! There are traffic cameras everywhere. All over the canopy. Whatever happened to that jaguar—"

"The traffic cameras would have caught it!" said Judy, excitedly, suddenly realizing what Nick meant.

"Bingo!" said Nick.

Judy chucked him on the arm, impressed. "Pretty sneaky, Slick."

"However. If you didn't have access to the system before, I doubt Chief Buffalo Butt is gonna give it to you now."

"No. But I've got a friend at city hall who might!" Judy smiled, feeling hopeful again.

18

It didn't take long for Judy and Nick to find Assistant Mayor Bellwether in city hall. She was struggling to hold a stack of files while keeping up with Mayor Lionheart.

"Sir?" said Bellwether. "If we could just review these very important—"

As Bellwether continued to struggle and dodge out of the way inside the busy lobby, she almost stepped on a little mouse.

"Oh, I'm sorry . . . sir!"

"I heard you, Bellwether," said Lionheart impatiently. "Just take care of it, okay?" He set a folder on top of her huge stack. "And clear my afternoon. I'm going out."

"But, sir, you have a meeting with Herds and Grazing. . . . Sir—"

Lionheart continued through the door, letting it

slam right in Bellwether's face. All the files she was carrying were knocked to the floor.

"Oh, mutton chops," she said, trying to collect the scattered pieces of paper.

"Assistant Mayor Bellwether," said Judy, approaching her. "We need your help."

Bellwether led them to her tiny, cramped office. Judy and Nick looked around, surprised. Bellwether's office was actually a janitor's closet!

"We just need to get into the traffic camera database," Judy said as Bellwether typed on the keyboard of her computer.

Nick barely touched the wool puff on top of Bellwether's head and whispered, "Sooo fluffy!" He was mesmerized. "Sheep never let me this close—so fluffy—like cotton candy—"

"You can't touch that! Stop it!" scolded Judy, swatting his hand away as she tried to keep Bellwether from seeing Nick.

"Where to?" Bellwether asked as she pulled up traffic cameras for the whole city. She looked up at Judy, catching the rabbit in mid-swat.

"Rainforest District. Vine and Tujunga."

Nick and Judy shared a smiled. This time, Judy had pronounced *Tujunga* correctly.

"This is so exciting, actually. Well, you know, I never get to do anything this important," said Bellwether.

"You're the assistant mayor of Zootopia," said Judy.

"Oh, I'm more of a glorified secretary," said Bellwether. "I think Mayor Lionheart just wanted the sheep vote. . . . But he did get me that nice mug." She proudly pointed to a mug that read WORLD'S GREATEST ~~DAD~~ ASSISTANT MAYOR.

"Smellwether!" shouted Mayor Lionheart through the intercom.

Bellwether cringed as she got up. "Oh, that's a fun little name he uses. I called him Lionfart once. He didn't care for that." She pressed the button on the intercom. "Yes, sir?"

"I thought you were going to cancel my afternoon!" Lionheart yelled.

"Oh, dear . . . I better go. Let me know what you find. It was really nice for me to—"

"While we're young, Smellwether!" the mayor's voice boomed again as she opened the door and hurried out.

"Well, I'm gonna need a lint brush," said Nick.

"Oh shush," said Judy. "Okay. Traffic cameras. Tujunga, Tujunga . . . we're in."

Nick and Judy watched the footage onscreen. They saw Manchas acting wild, and then . . . a black van pulled up, skidding to a stop.

"Who are these guys?" Judy asked.

"Timber wolves. Look at these dum-dums."

They watched as wolves got out of the van and trapped Manchas with a net! Judy gasped, but Nick just shook his head.

"Bet you a nickel one of them's gonna howl," Nick said.

One of the wolves howled.

"There it is. What is with wolves and howling?" he asked.

"Howlers. Night howlers," said Judy. "That's what Manchas was afraid of—wolves! The wolves are the night howlers. If they took Manchas—"

"I bet they took Otterton, too," said Nick.

"All we've gotta do is find out where they went," said Judy, examining the footage. As the wolves drove off, they disappeared through a tunnel and didn't come out the other side. "Wait. Where'd they go?"

Nick squinted at the picture. "You know, if I wanted to avoid surveillance because I was doing something illegal—which I never have—I'd use the maintenance tunnel 6B, which would put them out . . ." Nick clicked over to another camera's footage, then another, and another . . . and then the wolves emerged in the van! "Right there."

"Look at you," Judy said, impressed. "Junior Detective. You know, I think you'd actually make a pretty good cop."

"How dare you," Nick said in mock horror, trying not to smile.

Judy clicked through some more surveillance videos, tracking the wolves through alleys and back roads. "They're heading out of town," she said. "Where does that road go?"

"It's one of two places: it's either that very, very scary old building . . . or a Beaver Renaissance Faire."

19

Nick and Judy found the mysterious road and followed it. They stopped and watched from a distance as a van drove past a gated checkpoint. Beyond the gate was a creepy old building called Cliffside Asylum that perched high on a cliff over the ocean.

"Why couldn't you be a Beaver Renaissance Faire?" Nick said quietly.

The two slowly ventured toward the asylum, sneaking up to the guarded gate. They could see two wolves stationed inside. Nick motioned that he was going to try and tiptoe past. He started off, but as he got closer, one of the wolves sniffed the air, picking up on his scent. Nick grabbed a piece of driftwood to use as a weapon as the wolf began searching for the source of the scent. But before the wolf could find Nick, a howl sounded in the distance, grabbing the wolf's attention. "Ooooooooo!"

It was Judy, hidden beneath the cliffs!

Hearing the sound, the wolf couldn't help but howl back.

Another guard approached and said sharply, "Quit it, Gary. You're gonna start a howl."

"I didn't start it. Ooooooooo!" said Gary.

Unable to control it, the other guard howled back. Soon more and more wolves joined in, howling away.

Judy whispered to Nick, "Come on!" They used the distraction to jump the fence and sneak by the guards.

"Clever bunny," said Nick, impressed.

As they scrambled over the slippery rocks, Nick nearly slid down a waterfall. They searched for a way into the building and spotted a large pipe. Climbing inside, they walked until they emerged in the asylum. The dark cavernous room was full of old, rusty medical equipment.

"Looks like this was a hospital," said Judy.

She shined her light down a corridor and saw a metal door at the other end. They walked toward it. "You know, after you," Nick said, motioning for her to open the door. "You're the cop."

Judy slowly pushed the door open to reveal a room with shiny, modern new medical equipment. They cautiously walked in and looked around.

Nick pointed to scratches crisscrossing the floor. "Claw marks?" Judy said, taking in the sight. There were deep grooves in the door, too.

Feeling a little scared and intimidated, Nick started to back up. "Yeah, huge, huge claw marks. But what kind of anima—" A growl interrupted him, and then a locked-up, savage tiger grabbed Nick and pulled him toward his cell. Judy yanked Nick away, freeing him from the tiger's grip.

Judy held up her flashlight and swiveled it around the room to reveal . . . dozens of eyes! They walked along looking at each of the locked-up animals before finding a jaguar on all fours, pacing his cell. "Mr. Manchas," said Judy.

They continued past three, four, five cells, until finally, in the last one, they found a feral otter. It was Emmitt Otterton!

"It's him," said Judy. "We found our otter." She turned and spoke to him gently. "Mr. Otterton, my name is Officer Judy Hopps. Your wife sent me to find you. We're gonna get you out of here now."

Otterton screeched and lunged toward the glass wall, as if trying to attack.

"Or not," said Nick, backing away. "Guess he's in

no rush to get home to the Mrs."

Judy looked down the corridor of cells, counting, "Eleven, twelve, thirteen, fourteen. Plus Manchas." She thought for a moment, then said, "Chief Bogo handed out fourteen missing mammal files. . . . All the missing mammals are right here!"

Click! A door started to open, so Nick and Judy quickly hid next to an empty cell. They heard footsteps approaching, and soon they could see someone. . . .

It was Mayor Lionheart!

"Enough!" said Lionheart. "I don't want excuses, Doctor, I want answers."

Lionheart looked serious, intense, and tired. Judy whipped out her phone and started recording as Lionheart talked to a badger doctor.

"Mayor Lionheart, please," said the doctor. "We're doing everything we can."

"Oh, I don't think you are," said Lionheart. "Because I got a dozen and a half animals here who've gone off-the-freaking-rails crazy, and you can't tell me why. I'd call that *awfully* far from *doing everything*."

"Sir, it may be time to consider their biology," said the doctor.

Otterton, in the cage behind them, slammed against the glass walls of his cell.

"Biology, Doctor? Spare me."

"We both know what they all have in common. We can't keep it a secret. We need to come forward," the doctor said.

Lionheart snarled and turned on the doctor. "What do you think will happen if the press gets ahold of this?"

"What does Chief Bogo think?" asked the doctor.

"Chief Bogo doesn't know. And we are going to keep it that way."

Brrring! Brrring! Judy's phone broke the silence. It was her parents calling.

Lionheart looked up, startled. "Someone's here!"

"Sir, you need to go now," said the doctor. "Security, sweep the area!"

Nick and Judy ran as an alarm blared throughout the asylum. Wolves swarmed the halls.

"Great, we're dead. That's it. I'm dead. You're dead. Everybody's dead," Nick declared.

"Can you swim?" Judy asked Nick, ducking into an empty cell and putting her phone into an evidence bag.

"What? Can I swim? Of course. Why?" Nick watched Judy dive into a large hippo toilet. He closed his eyes and jumped in after her.

They slid through the pipe, twisting this way and that until they finally shot out, cascading over a waterfall. After a gasp of air, Nick swam to the riverbank. But Judy was nowhere to be seen. "Carrots? Hopps? Judy!"

He sighed when her saw her emerge from the water, holding her bagged phone over her head. "We've got to tell Bogo."

20

An hour later, the ZPD burst into Lionheart's office.

"Mayor Lionheart, you are under arrest for the kidnapping and false imprisonment of innocent citizens," Judy said as she cuffed him.

"You don't understand!" shouted Lionheart. "I had to do it!"

"You have the right to remain silent," Judy continued.

"I did it for the city!" Lionheart exclaimed.

Later on, Bogo addressed the press. Behind him were posters of the savage animals—each one of them sporting a muzzle. "Ladies and gentlemammals," said Bogo. "Fourteen mammals went missing, and all fourteen have been found by our newest recruit, who will speak to you in a moment."

"I am so nervous," said Judy as she and Nick stood off to the side.

"Okay, Press Conference 101," said Nick. "You wanna look smart, answer their questions with your own rhetorical questions. Then answer that question. Okay like this, 'Was this a tough case? Yes. Yes, it was.'"

"You should be up there with me. We did this together," said Judy.

"Well, am I a cop? No. No, I'm not," answered Nick.

"Funny you should say that . . . because I've been thinking. It would be nice to have a partner," said Judy, handing Nick an application to the ZPD. She offered the carrot pen to him. "Here. In case you need something to write with."

Bellwether gestured to Judy to come up to the podium. "Officer Hopps, it's time."

Nick looked down at the application, clicked the pen, and began filling it out.

As Judy stepped up, Bogo saluted her. She saluted back, and then the reporters started shouting out her name and asking questions. Judy pointed to one of them. "What can you tell us about the animals that went savage?" the reporter asked.

"Well, the animals in question . . . Are they all different species? Yes. Yes, they are," said Judy, looking toward Nick.

Nick smiled and gave her a thumbs-up.

"Okay, what's the connection?" shouted another reporter.

"All we know is that they're all members of the predator family," said Judy.

Nick frowned. The press reacted. Again, they yelled questions all at once. Judy was surprised.

"So predators are the only ones going savage?" demanded one reporter.

"That is accurate," said Judy, hesitating before she spoke. "Yes."

"Why is that happening?" yelled several reporters.

"We still don't know—"

The crowd rumbled with disappointment.

"BUT, but, but . . . it may have something to do with biology," said Judy, surprised by the escalating tension in the room.

Murmurs rippled across the press and a reporter asked, "What do you mean by that?"

"A biological component. You know, something in their DNA," Judy said.

"In their DNA? Can you elaborate on that, please?"

"Yes," Judy nodded, as the crowd got louder. "Thousands of years ago . . . predators survived through their aggressive hunting instincts. For whatever reason, they're reverting back to their savage ways."

Her comment caused a big hubbub. Nick didn't like what he was hearing. Clawhauser looked up. He was feeling uncomfortable, too.

"Officer Hopps, could it happen again?" asked another reporter.

"It is possible," said Judy. "We must be vigilant. And we at the ZPD are prepared and are here to protect you."

The press suddenly went into an absolute frenzy, asking questions like "What is being done to prevent it?" and "Should all predators be quarantined?"

Bellwether stepped up, eager to put an end to the questions. "Uh, thank you, Officer Hopps. Uh, no more questions."

"Oh, okay . . . but . . . I . . . didn't—" Before Judy could say another word, Bellwether ushered her away.

Unsure of how she had done, Judy walked across the lobby to Nick. "That went so fast. I didn't get a chance to mention you or say anything about—"

"Oh, I think you said plenty," said Nick, interrupting her.

"What do you mean?" Judy asked, confused.

"Clearly there's a biological component," he said

sarcastically, repeating her words. "These predators may be reverting back to their primitive savage ways." He looked at her incredulously. "Are you serious?"

"I just stated the facts of the case," said Judy. "I mean, it's not like a bunny could go savage."

"No, but a fox could, huh?"

"Stop it, Nick! You're not like them."

"There's a *them* now?"

"You know what I mean. You're not that kind of predator."

Nick gestured at all the posters. "The kind that needs to be muzzled? The kind that makes you think you need to carry around fox repellent? Yeah, don't think I didn't notice that little item the first time we met."

Nick got angrier and angrier, "So, you scared of me? Think I might go nuts? Go savage? Think I might what . . . try to eat you?"

Nick lunged, like he was going to bite her, and she flinched. Automatically, she put her hand on the fox repellent.

"I knew it. Just when I thought somebody actually believed in me," Nick said calmly. Then he handed her back the application. "Probably best if you don't have a predator as a partner."

As he walked away, he took off the sticker badge, crumpled it up, and tossed it into the trash.

"Nick!" Judy called after him, but he went straight out the door.

Judy had broken their friendship, and she didn't know how to fix it.

21

After the press conference, a wedge was driven between the animals of Zootopia, and everyone was talking about it. There were conflicts and protests. The animals began to treat one another differently.

At one protest, Judy stood in the middle of the two opposing sides as they argued.

"Go back to the forest, predator!" a pig yelled.

"I'm from the savanna!" shouted a beaver.

As the divide between prey and predators grew, it was on every news station.

Pop star Gazelle rallied for peace. "The Zootopia I know is better than this. We don't just blindly assign blame. We don't know why these attacks keep happening, but it is irresponsible to label all predators as savages. We cannot let fear divide us. Please . . . give me back the Zootopia I love."

Judy felt exhausted by all the fighting—and she

also felt responsible. She rode the subway on her way into work. There she watched a mother bunny pull her child to her as a lion boarded the train, and Judy shook her head. Judy got off at the next stop and went into the hospital.

"That's not my husband," Mrs. Otterton said, as she and Judy watched Emmitt Otterton flail around like a madman inside a padded room.

Judy sighed, her face full of worry. But there was nothing she could do.

Even inside the ZPD lobby the news was on.

Bogo called to Judy. "Come on, Hopps. The new mayor wants to see us."

"The mayor? Why?" she asked.

"It would seem you've arrived," Bogo said.

As Judy followed Bogo, she saw Clawhauser packing up his desk. "Clawhauser? What're you doing?" she asked.

"Oh, they thought it would be better if a *predator* such as myself wasn't the first face you see when you walk into the ZPD. So they're moving me to Records downstairs. By the boiler," he said.

Judy's disappointment was evident on her face.

"Hopps. Now!" Bogo commanded.

Mayor Bellwether was behind her desk in her big new fancy office as Bogo and Judy sat down. In front of them was a pamphlet with a picture of a smiling Judy that read "ZPD, Put Your Trust in Us." Judy looked at it, confused. "I don't understand."

"Our city is ninety percent prey, Judy," said Bellwether. "And right now, they're just really scared. You're a hero to them. They trust you. And so that's why Chief Bogo and I want you to be the public face of the ZPD."

"I'm not—I'm not a hero," said Judy sadly. "I came here to make the world a better place, but I think I broke it."

"Don't give yourself so much credit, Hopps," said Bogo. "The world has always been broken. That's why we need good cops like you."

"With all due respect, sir, a good cop is supposed to serve and protect—help the city, not tear it apart," said Judy. She took off her badge and handed it to Bogo. "I don't deserve this badge."

"Hopps," said Bogo.

"Judy. This is what you've always wanted. Since you

were a kid . . . you can't quit . . . ," said Bellwether.

"Thank you for the opportunity," said Judy. Then she rushed out of the office.

22

At her family vegetable stand in Bunnyburrow, Judy bagged carrots for a customer. "Four dozen carrots," she said robotically. "Have a nice day."

Stu and Bonnie approached her, concerned. "Hey there, Jude—Jude the Dude, remember that one? How we doin'?" asked Stu.

"I'm fine."

"You are not fine. Your ears are droopy," said Bonnie.

"Why did I think I could make a difference?" Judy asked.

"Well, because you're a trier, that's why," said Stu.

"You've always been a trier," said Bonnie.

"Yeah. I tried, and I made life so much worse for so many innocent predators."

"Oh, not all of them, though," Stu said. "Speak of the devil. Right on time."

Beep! A horn blared as a bakery truck pulled up to the stand.

Judy's eyes widened. "Is that . . . Gideon Grey?"

The truck had a sign that read GIDEON GREY'S EPICUREAN BAKED DELIGHTS . . . MADE WITH HOPPS FAMILY FARM PRODUCE.

"Yep. It sure is," Stu nodded. "We work with him now."

"He's our partner! And we'd never have considered it had you not opened our minds," said Bonnie.

"That's right," said Stu. "Gid's turned into one of the top pastry chefs in the triboroughs."

The fox in question climbed out of his truck. "Gideon Grey," said Judy. "I'll be darned."

"Hey, Judy," said Gideon. "I'd like to say sorry for the way I behaved in my youth. I had a lot of self-doubt that manifested itself in the form of unchecked rage and aggression. I was a major jerk."

"I know a thing or two about being a jerk," said Judy.

"Anyhow, I brought you all these pies," said Gideon, holding them up. Kid bunnies ran across the field, beelining it for the pies.

"Hey, kids!" shouted Stu. "Don't run through the *Midnicampum holicithias*!"

"Now, there's a four-dollar word, Mr. H. My family always just called them night howlers," said Gideon.

Judy's ears pricked up. "What did you say?" she asked.

Stu gestured to the flowers growing on the edge of the crops. "Oh, Gid's talking about those flowers, Judy. I use them to keep bugs off the produce. But I don't like the little ones going near them on account of your Uncle Terry."

"Yeah, Terry ate one whole when we were kids and went completely nuts," said Bonnie.

"He bit the dickens out of your mother," added Stu.

"A bunny can go savage . . . ," said Judy, putting the pieces together.

"Savage? Well, that's a strong word," said Bonnie.

"There's a sizable divot in your arm. I'd call that savage," said Stu.

Judy stood still as the thoughts raced through her head. "Night howlers aren't wolves. They're flowers. The flowers are making the predators go savage. That's it. That's what I've been missing." She raced away, then turned back. "Keys! Keys! Keys! Hurry! Come on!" Stu tossed her the keys to his pickup truck and Judy jumped in. "Thank you, I love you, bye!"

She peeled out and raced toward Zootopia.

23

Judy found Nick sitting in a lawn chair under a dark, lonely bridge.

"Night howlers aren't wolves. They're toxic flowers. I think someone is targeting predators on purpose and making them go savage."

"Wow," said Nick. "Isn't that interesting." He got up and walked off, but Judy followed.

"Wait, listen! I know you'll never forgive me. And I don't blame you. I wouldn't forgive me, either. I was ignorant and irresponsible and small-minded. But predators shouldn't suffer because of my mistakes. I have to fix this, but I can't do it without you."

Nick sighed but still refused to look at her.

"And after we're done, you can hate me, and that'll be fine, because I was a horrible friend and I hurt you. . . . And you can walk away knowing you were right all along, I really am just a dumb bunny."

Nick didn't respond. It was awkwardly quiet until, suddenly, Judy's voice played back on a recorder. "I really am just a dumb bunny. I really am just a dumb bunny."

Nick emerged from the shadows, holding up her carrot pen. "Cheer up, Carrots. I'll let you erase it . . . in forty-eight hours."

Judy's eyes welled up with tears. Nick shook his head. "All right, get in here."

She put her arms around Nick and hugged him tightly.

"You bunnies are so emotional," said Nick. "Are you just trying to steal the pen? Is that what this is? You are standing on my tail, though. Off, off, off."

Nick and Judy climbed into the pickup truck.

"Oh! I thought you guys only grew carrots!" said Nick, grabbing a basket of blueberries and popping a few into his mouth. "What's the plan?"

"We're gonna follow the night howlers. Know this guy?" Judy asked, holding up a picture of Duke Weaselton, the crook Judy had busted in Little Rodentia for stealing flower bulbs.

"I know everybody," said Nick.

24

Judy and Nick found Weaselton standing on a street corner, selling random junk. "Anything you need . . . I got it," he called. "All your favorite movies! I got movies that haven't even been released yet!" In front of him were knock-off movies like *Wreck-It Rhino*, *Wrangled*, and *Pig Hero 6*.

"Well, well, look who's back in the bootleg business," Nick said, walking up to him.

"What's it to you, Wilde? Shouldn't you be melting down a pawpsicle or something?" Weaselton recognized Judy. "Hey, if it isn't Flopsy the Copsy."

"We both know those weren't moldy onions I caught you stealing," said Judy. "What were you going to do with those night howlers, Wezzleton?"

"It's Weaselton! Duke Weaselton. And I ain't talking, rabbit. And ain't nothing you can do to make me." He flicked a toothpick in her face. Judy turned to Nick and smiled. She knew they had the exact same idea.

Not long after, polar bears held Weaselton over the icy death pit inside Mr. Big's place. "Ice 'im," said Mr. Big.

Weaselton screamed and squirmed, trying to break free. "You dirty rat! Why you helping her? You know she's a cop!"

Mr. Big motioned for his polar bears to wait as they dangled Weaselton over the pit. "And the godmother to my future granddaughter."

Fru Fru emerged from the other room, showing off her pregnant belly. "I'm going to name her Judy," said Fru Fru happily.

"Aw," said Judy.

"Ice this weasel," Mr. Big ordered.

"Wait! Stop! I'll talk!" screamed Weaselton. "I stole them night howlers because I could sell them for a lot of dough."

"And to whom did you sell them?" asked Judy.

"A ram named Doug. We got a drop spot underground. Just watch it. Doug ain't exactly friendly."

25

Nick and Judy followed Weaselton's instructions and found the drop: an old subway car in an abandoned station. They hid as two tough rams exited the car.

Once the rams were gone, Nick lifted Judy and she pushed open the window to peek inside. "The weasel wasn't lying," she whispered as she climbed through.

The interior of the car had been transformed into a greenhouse. There were rows upon rows of night howlers. "Yeah, looks like old Doug's cornered the market on night howlers," said Nick.

Click! A door opened, and Judy and Nick quickly hid under a desk. They watched as a ram wearing a lab coat with the name DOUG on it entered and stood over the flowering plants. He carefully harvested the pollen and produced a small blue paint ball–like pellet of serum. Nick and Judy watched in disbelief.

Doug's phone rang and he held it to his ear. "Yeah?

What's the mark? Cheetah in Sahara Square. Got it." Doug loaded the pellet into his gun and cocked it. A map with pictures of various animal targets was on the wall behind him. "Yeah, I know they're fast. I can hit him. Listen, I hit a tiny little otter through the open window of a moving car," he said.

Judy and Nick shared a look. It was suddenly clear. The map contained the images of all the missing animals. The ram must have hit them with the serum from the night howlers, turning them all savage.

"Yeah, I'll buzz you when it's done. Or you'll see it on the news. You know, whichever comes first."

Bam! Bam! The two rams banged on the door.

"Hey, Doug, open up," said one of the rams.

Doug finished his call and let them in.

Wham! Suddenly, Judy kicked Doug in the back, knocking him into the rams. With them on the other side of the door, she locked it, shutting them out.

"What are you doing?" shouted Nick.

The rams surrounded the subway car and pounded on the doors from outside.

"We need to get this evidence to the ZPD," said Judy.

"Okay. Got it," said Nick, picking up the case.

"No. All of it," said Judy, smiling.

"Wait, what?" Nick said. "You're a conductor now? Listen. It would take a miracle to get this rust bucket going."

She fired up the engine of the subway car and they started to move.

"Oh, hallelujah," Nick said in defeat.

The train gained speed and began to race down the tracks. Nick finally allowed himself to smile.

"Mission accomplished. Would it be premature for me to do a little victory toot-toot?" Nick gestured to the train whistle.

"All right," said Judy. "One toot-toot."

Toot! Toot! Nick happily blew the train whistle.

Bam! One of the rams burst into the car through the door. The train slowed down as Nick and Judy tried to push him out. Nick managed to get the door closed, but the ram continued to bang up against it.

Bam! Bam! Bam! The other ram appeared on the windshield and headbutted it. "Maybe that's just hail?" Nick joked.

Boom! He finally managed to bust through the windshield and knocked Judy out the window! She grabbed on to his horns as the subway car continued chugging down the track.

"Speed up, Nick! Speed up!" she shouted.

"Are you crazy? There's another train coming!"

"Trust me! SPEED! UP!"

A split second before the trains crashed into each other, Judy kicked the ram into a track-switch lever, and the train car they were riding in changed tracks!

Then the subway car derailed, and Judy and Nick dove out onto a platform. The car exploded, and all its contents, including the night howlers, burned to a crisp.

"Everything's gone. We lost it all," said Judy.

Nick held up the case containing a gun and a pellet. "Yeah," he said, "except for this."

26

Nick and Judy came up the stairs from the subway and raced through the empty Natural History Museum on their way to the ZPD. All around them were statues and exhibits telling about the history of the evolution of Zootopia.

"There it is!" Judy said. She could see the ZPD offices through the exit doors of the museum.

"Judy! Judy!" a voice called.

They stopped and turned to see Bellwether standing behind them with two sheep cops.

"Mayor Bellwether!" Judy said. "We found out what's happening. Someone's darting predators with a serum—that's what's making them go savage."

"I am so proud of you, Judy. You did such a super job," said Bellwether, applauding.

"Thank you, ma'am. . . . How did you know where to find us?" asked Judy.

"I'll go ahead and take that case now," said Bellwether.

Something about the way Bellwether was acting made Judy suspicious. "You know what? I think Nick and I will just take this to the ZPD. . . ."

Judy turned to go, but the sheep blocked their way. Why wouldn't Bellwether let them leave? All of a sudden, it became crystal clear to Judy. Bellwether was the one behind this from the very beginning! That was why she had known where they would be. Judy signaled to Nick and they dashed off down a corridor as Bellwether shouted, "Get them!"

While she and Nick were running as fast as they could toward the police department, Judy glanced over her shoulder. She didn't see the woolly mammoth tusk sticking out in front of her, and ran right into it. Judy screamed in pain as the tusk slashed her leg and knocked her off her feet.

"Carrots!" shouted Nick.

Nick rushed to her. Her leg was bleeding badly. He carried her behind a pillar. "I got you, come here. Okay, but just relax." A few blueberries rolled out from Nick's pocket. "Blueberry?" he asked, offering one to Judy.

"Pass," she said.

"Come on out, Judy!" called Bellwether.

"Take the case," Judy whispered passing it to Nick.

"Get it to Bogo."

"I'm not going to leave you behind. That's not happening," said Nick.

"I can't walk," said Judy.

"Just . . . we'll think of something," said Nick.

"We're on the same team, Judy!" said Bellwether, trying to get Judy to surrender. "Underestimated. Underappreciated," she went on. "Aren't you sick of it? Predators—they may be strong and loud, but prey outnumber predators ten to one. Think about it: ninety percent of the population, united against a common enemy. We'll be unstoppable."

Bellwether spotted the shadow of long rabbit ears against the wall and gestured to the sheep. They pounced, but it was just a mummified jackalope. Judy and Nick made a run for it.

"Over there!" Bellwether shouted.

Whack! A sheep tackled them, knocking the case out of Nick's grip and sending them both into a sunken diorama. Bellwether looked over the edge from above.

"What are you going to do?" asked Judy. "Kill me?"

"Of course not . . . *he* is," said Bellwether, gesturing to Nick. She took the dart gun out of the case and aimed at Nick. *Thwick!* The dart sank into Nick's skin.

"No! Nick!" Judy yelled.

Nick started to shake and crouched over as Bellwether dialed her phone.

"Yes, police!" Bellwether said into the phone. "There's a savage fox in the Natural History Museum. Officer Hopps is down! Please hurry!"

Judy searched for a way out of the diorama, but there was nowhere to go. Nick, now on all fours, looked like a wild animal. "No. Nick," said Judy. "Don't do this. Fight it."

"Oh, but he can't help it, can he?" said Bellwether. "Since preds are just *biologically* predisposed to be savages."

Nick stalked Judy like a predator about to attack as she helplessly tried to limp away.

"Gosh, think of the headline: 'Hero Cop Killed by Savage Fox,'" said Bellwether, pleased with herself.

"So that's it? Prey fears predator, and you stay in power?" asked Judy.

"Pretty much," said Bellwether.

"It won't work," said Judy.

"Fear always works," said Bellwether. "And I'll dart every predator in Zootopia to keep it that way."

Nick growled as he cornered Judy.

"Bye-bye, bunny," said Bellwether.

Nick lunged at Judy. Bellwether smiled.

"Blood, blood, blood!" shouted Judy. "And death."

Bellwether looked on, completely confused.

Nick stood up and helped Judy to her feet.

"All right, you know, you're milking it. Besides, I think we got it, I think we got it. We got it up there, thank you, yakety yak—you laid it all out beautifully," Nick said.

"What?" Bellwether said, trying to figure out what was going on.

Nick held up the ball of serum, then gestured to the gun. "Yeah," he said. "Oh, are you looking for the serum? Well, it's right here."

"What you've got in the weapon there—those are blueberries. From my family's farm," said Judy.

"They are delicious. You should try some."

Nick licked his fingers.

Bellwether looked down to see a blueberry in the chamber of the dart gun.

"I framed Lionheart, I can frame you! It's my word against yours!" she yelled angrily.

Nick held the carrot pen up high into the air so that Bellwether could see it.

"Oh, yeah, actually . . . ," Judy started.

Nick pressed a button on the pen, and Bellwether's

voice played back: "And I'll dart every predator in Zootopia to keep it that way. . . ."

". . . it's your word against yours," said Judy.

Judy and Nick looked at one another and smiled. "It's called a hustle, sweetheart," they said together.

27

The next day, all the news channels aired footage of Bellwether in an orange jumpsuit, being led to jail.

"Former mayor Dawn Bellwether is behind bars today, guilty of masterminding the savage attacks that have plagued Zootopia of late," said a newscaster.

The footage showed Lionheart being led *out* of prison.

"Her predecessor, Leodore Lionheart, denies any knowledge of her plot, claiming he was just trying to protect the city," the newscaster said. "A reporter interviewed Lionheart from jail."

"Did I falsely imprison those animals? Well, yes. Yes, I did. Classic 'doing the wrong thing for the right reason' scenario. Know what I mean, Kitty?"

"No. No, I do not," answered the reporter, deadpan.

Back in the studio, the newscaster continued. "In related news, doctors say the night howler antivenom is proving effective in rehabilitating all of the victims."

When Mr. Otterton awoke inside the hospital, his wife was hugging him tightly. Judy was there, watching and smiling.

"Thank you," said Mrs. Otterton gratefully.

Months later, Judy stood proudly at a lectern giving the commencement address to graduates of the Zootopia Police Academy.

"When I was a kid, I thought Zootopia was this perfect place where everyone got along and anyone could be anything. . . . Turns out, real life's a little bit more complicated than a slogan on a bumper sticker. Real life is messy. We all have limitations. We all make mistakes, which means . . . hey, glass half full! We all have a lot in common. And the more we try to understand one another, the more exceptional each of us will be. But we have to try. No matter what type of animal you are, from the biggest elephant to our first fox, I implore you: Try. Try to make a difference. Try to make the world better. Try to look inside yourself and recognize that change starts with you. It starts with me. It starts with all of us."

Nick approached the stage. He stood tall in front of her, his chest out. Judy pinned on his badge.

The crowd went wild with applause as cadets threw

their caps high up into the air.

"All right! Enough! Shut it!" said Chief Bogo.

Judy and Nick took their seats among the other cops in the bullpen. Bogo stood up at the front, calling order. "We have some new recruits with us this morning," said Bogo. "Including our first fox. But . . . who cares?"

"You should have your own line of inspirational greeting cards, sir," said Nick sarcastically.

"Shut your mouth, Wilde," said Bogo, then began calling out assignments. When he finally got to Judy and Nick, they waited eagerly. "Hopps, Wilde . . . Skunk Pride Parade. Dismissed."

"Fun," said Nick. "Funny guy."

"Parade detail is a step up from parking duty," Judy said.

Bogo looked as if he was going to smile . . . but then he didn't.

28

"**S**o are all rabbits bad drivers, or is it just you?" asked Nick.

Judy slammed on the brakes, causing Nick to lurch forward, accidentally jamming his pawpsicle into his face.

"Oops. Sorry," she said.

"Sly bunny," said Nick, wiping his face.

"Dumb fox."

"Come on, you know I love you," said Nick.

"Do I know that? Yes. Yes, I do."

Judy and Nick smiled at each other. Suddenly, a tricked-out red sports car blasted past them going over a hundred miles per hour. Their smiles got even wider, and Nick hit the siren. *Bwoop! Bwoop!* Judy stomped on the gas and they took off, chasing after the sports car, catching air along the way.